THAT'S WHAT
I THOUGHT

BY **ALICE SCHERTLE**

ILLUSTRATED BY **JOHN WALLNER**

HARPER & ROW, PUBLISHERS • NEW YORK

Library of Congress Cataloging-in-Publication Data

Schertle, Alice.
    That's what I thought.

    Summary: A little girl imagines different, exciting,
and dangerous situations and is comforted by her parents'
loving reassurance.
    [1. Imagination—Fiction.   2. Parent and child—
Fiction]   I. Wallner, John C., ill.   II. Title.
PZ7.S3442Tj   1990   [E]   88-922
ISBN 0-06-025204-9
ISBN 0-06-025205-7 (lib. bdg.)

This one's for Jenny
—A.S.

To Linda Zuckerman
with sincere thanks and affection
—J.C.W.

It was a rainy afternoon. Imogene sat by the window watching raindrops slide down the glass. Tiger Cat was curled up on the sofa beside her.

"What if it never stopped raining?" asked Imogene.

"It will stop," Mama told her, "sooner or later."

"But what if it never did?" said Imogene. "What if it rained and rained, and all the cars floated away, and water came into the house up to the ceiling?"

A clap of thunder made the lamps rattle. Daddy
picked up Tiger Cat and sat down next to Imogene.
"There's only one thing to do when it rains that much,"
he said. "We'd have to make a boat out of this sofa.
We'd use the broom for a mast and your bedspread for
a sail."

"How would we eat?" asked Imogene.

Mama sat down too. "We'd sail past the market and fish for groceries."

"What would Tiger Cat do?" Imogene wanted to know.

"She could sit on top of the mast," Daddy said, "and look out for sharks."

"Would there be sharks?" asked Imogene.
Daddy said, "You never know."
Thunder rumbled overhead.

"Daddy," said Imogene, "will it really rain forever
and ever?"

"No," said Daddy. "The rain will stop. You'll go
outside and walk in the puddles."

"And when you come back in," said Mama, "I'll tell
you to take off your muddy boots."

"That's what I thought," said Imogene.

One evening, Imogene asked Mama, "What would you do if a bear came to our house and wanted to eat me up?"

"I'd lock the door," said Mama.

"What if he came in the window?"

"In that case," said Mama, "I'd make him a big dinner."

"Then he'd be too full to eat me up," said Imogene.

"Much too full," Mama agreed. "Unless he still wanted dessert."

Imogene thought about that. "What if you didn't have any dessert to give him?"

"Well, in that case," Mama said, "I'd just have to put you on a pie plate with a dollop of whipped cream on your head."

Imogene felt the top of her head. "Would you really feed me to the bear? I mean *really*?"

"No," said Mama. "That old bear would have to be content with yesterday's doughnuts. And if he growled for more, I'd swat him with the broom."

"That's what I thought," said Imogene.

A few days later, Daddy and Imogene were working in the garden.

"Daddy," said Imogene as she pulled the hose over to the melon patch, "what would you do if this watermelon grew and grew? What if it grew as big as I am?"

"I believe I'd stop watering it," said Daddy.

Imogene thought about that. "But what if it kept growing anyway? What if it grew as big as the house?"

"There's only one way to deal with a melon that size," said Daddy. "I'd cut a door in it with the chain saw. We'd back in the pickup truck and scoop out the insides. Then we'd be eating watermelon for a very long time."

"What about the seeds?" asked Imogene.

"We could use them for stepping-stones," said Daddy.

Imogene said, "What about the shell?"

"I'd cut that in half," Daddy told her. "We'd fill half with water and use it for a swimming pool."

Imogene bent down and saw a green melon
nestled among the vines. "What if it doesn't grow big
enough?"

"Well then," said Daddy, "you and Mama and I will
just have a nice piece of cool, juicy watermelon."

"That's what I thought," said Imogene.

One warm summer day, Mama and Imogene went fishing. Imogene put a small marshmallow on her hook. She tossed the line into the water and watched the marshmallow sink out of sight.

"What if I hooked a whale?" asked Imogene.

"He'd never fit in the frying pan," said Mama.

"But what would you do," Imogene wanted to know, "if I really caught a whale?"

"Well," said Mama, "I'd take the hook out of his mouth, but only if he promised to take us for a ride. You and I would climb up on his back, and away we'd go."

"All the way to China?" asked Imogene.

"Certainly," said Mama. "And on the way home we'd
have a race with every ship we saw."
"And beat them all!" cried Imogene.
"Right," said Mama. "All except the pirate ship."

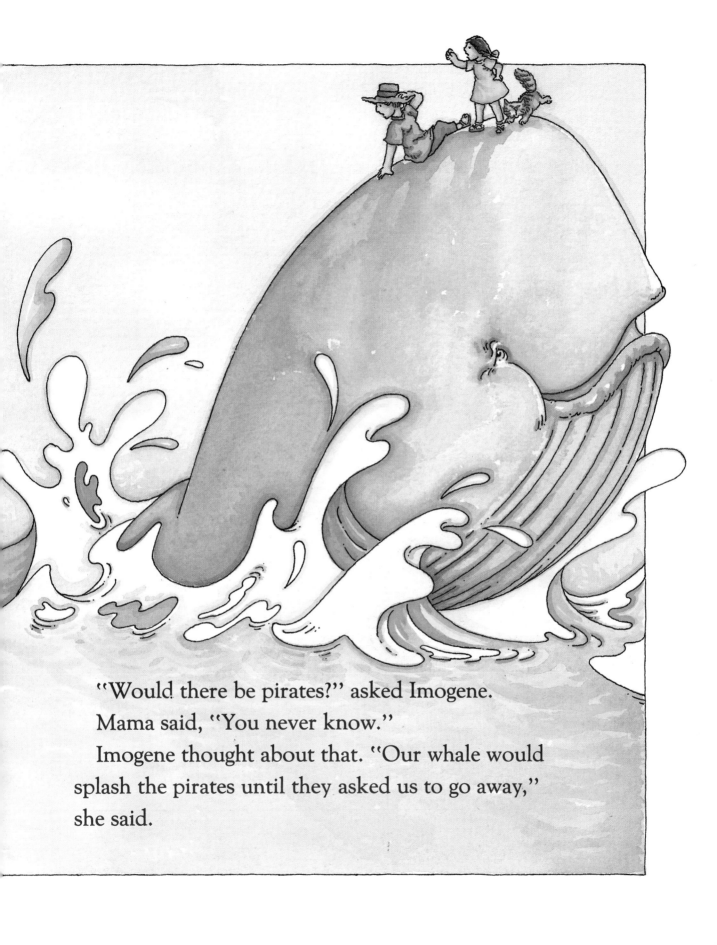

"Would there be pirates?" asked Imogene.

Mama said, "You never know."

Imogene thought about that. "Our whale would splash the pirates until they asked us to go away," she said.

Suddenly, Imogene felt a tug on her line. The end of her pole dipped into the water. "Mama!" she shouted. "I think I hooked something!"

"Good girl," said Mama. "This one will fit in the frying pan."

"That's what I thought," said Imogene.

One night, on the way to bed, Imogene said, "What would you do if I were really naughty and wouldn't stop?"

"Oh, we'd sell you to someone who wanted a naughty child," said Mama.

"Who would buy a naughty child?" asked Imogene.

"Maybe someone who didn't like visitors," Daddy told her. "Someone might want to keep a naughty child to scare people away from the door."

Imogene laughed. "How much would you sell me for?"

"About a nickel."

"Would you really sell me?" Imogene wanted to know. "I mean *really*?"

"Not for a million dollars," said Daddy.

"Not for the sun and the moon and all of the stars," said Mama.

"That's what I thought," said Imogene.